*For all kids who only need a rag and an old
shirt in order to set off to Beh-tel-helm*
—Annette Langen

For Mees and Liv
—Marije Tolman

Our Very Own
Christmas

Annette Langen & Marije Tolman

NorthSouth
New York / London

Yes, indeed, Kelly knows all the things that happened
on Christmas. For when it gets dark outside, she likes
to be Mary. And her little brother, Franklin, always
gets to be Joseph.

And when they are Mary and Joseph, they always set
out on the long journey to Bethlehem.

"Well, Joseph, we should be on our way," Mary would say. "Just the two of us and our little donkey." And as they have no donkey, a little sheep comes along.

Little Joseph would nod. "Yes, Mary. Let's be on our way," he would say.

And so the two of them would start their journey and travel far, very far . . . through the darkest night . . . farther and farther. . . . Far, far away their journey takes them . . . until finally they can see the lights of a city. . . .

"Behold, it is Bethlehem!" Mary would say, awfully relieved.

Little Joseph nods his head solemnly and confirms, "Yes, there it is, Beh-tel-helm!"

Then he's usually at a loss.

"What's next, Kelly?" he whispers.

"I would be Mary, though," says Kelly. "We would have to find shelter for the night. The baby will come soon!"

"Ah, yes," little Joseph says, and he goes, "*Knock, knock!* Do you have room for us?" he asks.
Then little Joseph shakes his head and sadly announces, "No. There is no room!"

"Knock on the next door!" says Mary.
So little Joseph goes again, "*Knock, knock!
Do you have room for us?*"
And again he shakes his head sadly and says,
"No. There is no room here either!"

"Let's try back there as well," Kelly tells him.

And for the third time he goes, "*Knock, knock! Do you have room for us?*"

But again he just shakes his head and very sadly says, "No. There is no room."

At that point Mary cries out desperately, "There is no room for us anywhere!"

And little Joseph never remembers what he is supposed to say next.

"Oh, woe. Oh, woe."

Mary whispers to him softly. And little Joseph exclaims with feeling, "Oh, woe! Oh, woe!"

And it sounds very, very sad.

Here, Mary gets up.

"Yet we are lucky. A nice lady said to us, 'There is room for you in our barn. It's right there, in the back.'"

And little Joseph nods. "Let's go, Kelly," he says.

"But I would be Mary!" Kelly says firmly.

"Let's go!" cries little Joseph, and he takes Mary by the hand and leads her to the barn.

There are animals in the stable.

"Hi there, ox! Hello, dear sheep!" little Joseph greets them.

And little Mary yawns. "I would be so tired, I would lay myself down on the straw," she says. "But the animals would have kept me warm."

Little Joseph nods and lies down as well.

Suddenly Mary jumps up. "And then later I would
have shouted, 'Joseph, our baby, baby Christ is here!'"
    And now little Joseph gets to hold baby Christ in
his arms.
    "We will name him Jesus!" says Mary, and gently
kisses the newborn baby Christ.

Little Joseph knows what's next.
"There is a big star in the sky, shining ever so brightly!"
he says, and points upward.

Little Mary nods.
"Yes, and all the angels would sing," she says.
"Because they are rejoicing that little baby Jesus is born."

Little Joseph sits down.

"There will be visitors, many, many visitors." He is very positive about that.

And there it goes:

"*Knock! Knock!*"

"Who is there?" little Joseph asks in a deep voice.

Then Mary exclaims, "It's the angels! They will be spreading the news everywhere that our Christ child was born."

Little Joseph nods.
"That is good. Bye-bye, angels!"

Oh, then he has to think. ". . . and what happens now?" he asks.

And Mary whispers, "*Knock, knock!*"

"Ah, yes!" little Joseph exclaims, and quickly goes, "*Knock! Knock!*"

"Welcome, dear shepherds!" Mary exclaims.

"What beautiful presents you bring for our baby Jesus! Lovely soft wool, tasty milk, and even a little lamb . . . Thank you very much!"

Mary has barely finished when there is another knock.

"*Knock-knock! Knock-knock! Knock-knock!*"

Little Mary is very surprised: "Who might this be?" she asks.

Little Joseph, though, he knows. "It's the three kings! Hello!"

Little Mary exclaims, "Oh, you have brought such beautiful presents: gold, franklin sense, and something else. . . . Little baby Jesus will be ever so happy."

Little Joseph nods and whispers, "And now?"

Very content, little Mary says, "Then everybody would go home again. You, Joseph, and I, we would be sleeping in the barn. With only the star shining brightly above us. For the angels are taking good care of sweet little baby Christ."

"Super!" little Joseph says.

"So there you see," says Kelly, putting down her blue scarf, "all the things that happened on Christmas."

"Hmmm . . . ," Franklin says happily, ". . . and tomorrow we will go to Beh-tel-helm again."